Rose and Riley

Jane Cutler

Pictures by Thomas F. Yezerski

To Leah,
Have a happy unbirthday!
Thomas F. Yezerski

Farrar Straus Giroux

New York

For David Holton
—J.C.

For Matt and Mary Beth
—T.F.Y.

Text copyright © 2005 by Jane Cutler
Illustrations copyright © 2005 by Thomas F. Yezerski
All rights reserved
Distributed in Canada by Douglas & McIntyre Publishing Group
Color separations by Chroma Graphics PTE Ltd.
Printed and bound in the United States of America by Phoenix Color Corporation
Designed by Jay Colvin
First edition, 2005
10 9 8 7 6 5 4 3 2 1

www.fsgkidsbooks.com

Library of Congress Cataloging-in-Publication Data
Cutler, Jane.
    Rose and Riley / Jane Cutler ; pictures by Thomas F. Yezerski— 1st ed.
        p.   cm.
    Summary: Together, two good friends figure out how to prepare for the possibility of
rain, how to celebrate un-birthdays, and what to do with worries.
    ISBN-13: 978-0-374-36340-6
    ISBN-10: 0-374-36340-4
    [1. Best friends—Fiction. 2. Friendship—Fiction. 3. Life skills—Fiction.] I. Yezerski,
Thomas, ill. II. Title.

PZ7.C985Ro 2005
[E]—dc22

                                                                                    2003054887

Contents

Rose and Riley

Rose and her friend Riley
were ready for rain.
Rose had a red umbrella.
Riley's was green.
"We are ready for rain," Rose said.

Riley looked outside Rose's window.

The sun was shining. The sky was blue.

"I am closing my umbrella," said Riley.

"When it rains, I will open it."

"It is good to be ready," said Rose.

Riley looked outside again.

The sun was still shining.

The sky was still blue.

Riley put away his umbrella.

Rose and Riley went outside.

The sun made Riley feel happy.

The sun shining on her umbrella

made Rose feel hot.

The blue sky made Riley feel happy.

Rose could not see the blue sky.

"Close your umbrella, Rose," said Riley,

"so you can see the sky."

"I want to be ready," said Rose.

So Riley played in the sun
under the blue sky.
And Rose waited for rain
under her umbrella.

After a while, Riley got tired
of playing by himself.
After a while, Rose got tired
of waiting by herself.
"We could go for a walk," Riley said.

Riley and Rose walked by the lake.

Riley skipped stones on the water.

Rose held her umbrella.

Riley was happy.

Rose was ready.

Then Riley saw a cloud.

"Look, Rose," he said.

"That looks like a rain cloud," said Rose.

"It is a rain cloud," said Riley.

Soon Rose and Riley heard a drop of rain
fall into the lake. *Plonk!*
They heard a drop
fall onto the umbrella. *Plat!*
"I am ready!" cried Rose.
"It is time to go home!" said Riley.

"You can walk under my umbrella
with me," said Rose.
But the red umbrella was small.
No matter which way Rose and Riley turned,
one of them did not fit all the way under it.

Then Riley put his arm around Rose.

Rose tried to put her arm around Riley.

They both held the umbrella.

Home they went.

After the rain stopped,

the sun came out.

The sky was blue.

"Next time," Riley said,

"I will take my umbrella. I will be ready."

"Next time," Rose said,

"I will leave my umbrella at home.

I will play in the sun.

I will skip stones on the water."

"But what if it rains?" said Riley.

"Then *I* will share *your* umbrella," said Rose.

The Un-Birthday Party

"Tomorrow is my un-birthday," said Rose.

"What does that mean?" asked Riley.

"It means it is not my birthday," said Rose.

"And I am going to have an un-birthday party here at my house."

"What is an un-birthday party like?"
asked Riley.

"An un-birthday party is fun," said Rose.

"You have cake and ice cream."

"I like cake and ice cream!" said Riley.

"You have soda pop," said Rose.

"I like soda pop!" said Riley.

"You have games," said Rose.

"I like games!" said Riley.

"You have presents," said Rose.

"I like presents!" said Riley.

"Everyone sings 'Happy Un-Birthday to
  You,'" said Rose.
"An un-birthday party sounds
  just like a birthday party," said Riley.
"It *is* just like a birthday party," said Rose.
"Except you have it on your un-birthday."

"Rose," Riley said, "tomorrow
is my un-birthday, too.
And I've decided to have
an un-birthday party."
"You cannot," said Rose.

"Why?" said Riley.

"Because I am having one," said Rose.

"But, Rose," Riley said, "my un-birthday
  is just like your un-birthday.
  If I want to have an un-birthday party,
  I can have one."

"Riley," said Rose, "what would happen
  if everyone had an un-birthday party
  on their un-birthdays?"
"We would have a lot of parties!" said Riley.
"Maybe too many," said Rose.

"You cannot have too many parties!" said Riley.

"I do not know. Let me think," said Rose.

"Think about what?" Riley said.

"About what it would be like

if everyone had an un-birthday party."

"There would be a party every day!"
said Riley.

"And what would we do for birthdays?"
asked Rose.

"We would have *birthday* parties!" said Riley.

"What would they be like?" asked Rose.

"They would be just like un-birthday parties!"
Riley said.

"But if there is already a party every day,
what would make your birthday special?"
said Rose.

Riley thought. Rose thought.

"Um—*no* party?" said Riley.

"No party," said Rose.

"I do not like that," said Riley.

"I do not like that, either," said Rose.

"Maybe an un-birthday party should not
  be just like a birthday party," said Riley.

"What should an un-birthday party be like?"
  said Rose.

"No cake?" said Riley. "No soda pop?
  No presents? No games? No songs?"

"No party," said Rose.

"Right," said Riley. "No un-birthday party."

The Worry Dolls

"I am worried," said Rose.

"Worried?" said Riley.

"I am worried," said Rose, "and I am tired."

"Tired?" said Riley.

"I am worried when I go to bed.

Then I cannot sleep.

So I am tired," said Rose.

"What are you worried about?" asked Riley.

"I am worried about everything," said Rose.

"Everything!" said Riley.

"No wonder you cannot sleep!"

Riley did not want Rose to be worried.

What could he do?

"Rose," said Riley, "I will cook for you."

"I do not want to eat," said Rose.

"Rose," said Riley,

"I will help you paint your house."

"I do not want to paint," said Rose.

"Rose," said Riley, "I will take you
to the zoo."

"I do not want to go," said Rose.

"Rose," said Riley, "you do not want
to do anything!"

Now Riley was worried.

Rose always liked to do things.

Riley went home.

What could he do to help Rose?

"I know!" Riley said. "I will make Rose

some worry dolls.

The worry dolls can worry,

and Rose can stop."

Riley got out ten flat toothpicks

and a tiny white box.

He got out a black pen.

He got out his sewing kit.

At one end of each toothpick

Riley made two eyes and a mouth.

He made black hair.

Then he covered each toothpick
with different-colored thread.
Yellow. Blue. Orange. Red.
Green. Purple. Gold.
Brown. Black. White.

Riley made ten tiny dolls.

He put them into the tiny box.

He ran back.

"Rose! Rose!" he called.

"I have something for you."

Riley gave the tiny box to Rose.

Rose looked inside.

"What did you make?" she asked.

"I made worry dolls," said Riley.

"What are worry dolls?" asked Rose.

"Worry dolls are dolls
you tell your worries to," said Riley.

"When?" asked Rose.

"At night," said Riley.

"When you want to go to sleep.
You tell one worry to each doll.
The doll worries and you do not.
You go to sleep."

"And what about the worry dolls?"
   asked Rose.

"What *about* the worry dolls?" said Riley.

"When do they sleep?" said Rose.

"They sleep while you
   do all the things you like to do.

Then they stay awake and worry for you

so you can sleep and be not-worried

and not-tired again the next day."

Rose took the tiny dolls out of the tiny box.

She smiled.

"It just might work, Riley," she said.

"It just might," said Riley.